For Matthew, Charlie, Jack, and Sally

Text copyright © 1993 by Catherine and Laurence Anholt

All rights reserved.

First U.S. edition 1993
Published in Great Britain in 1993 by Walker Books Ltd., London.

Library of Congress Cataloging-in-Publication Data

Anholt, Catherine.
Here come the babies / Catherine and Laurence Anholt.
Summary: Rhyming text, from the perspective of older siblings,
describes the characteristics and behavior of babies.
ISBN 1-56402-209-9
1. Infants—Juvenile literature. [1. Babies.   2. Brothers and sisters.]
I. Anholt, Laurence.   II. Title.
HQ774.A67   1993
305.23'2—dc20   92-54584

10 9 8 7 6 5 4 3 2 1

Printed in Italy.

The pictures in this book were done in watercolor and ink.

Candlewick Press
2067 Massachusetts Avenue
Cambridge, Massachusetts 02140

Here come the
BABIES

Catherine and Laurence Anholt

CANDLEWICK PRESS
CAMBRIDGE, MASSACHUSETTS

Here come the babies!

Babies in boxes, babies in boots, babies on backs.

Babies in socks, babies in suits, babies in packs.

Babies everywhere!

Babies in coats, babies in cribs, babies with cats.

Babies in boats, babies in bibs, babies with bats.

What are babies like?

Babies kick and babies crawl,

Slide their potties down the hall.

Babies smile and babies yell,

This one has a funny smell.

What do babies look like?

Wriggles and dribbles and sticking-out ears,

Little round faces with rivers of tears.

Babies wear suits which are long at the toes,

They stick out in the middle and up at the nose.

What are mornings like?

Mom and Dad are fast asleep
And all the house is quiet.
I slip into baby's room
And start a little riot.

What are mealtimes like?

Baby throwing tantrums,
Baby throwing fits,
Baby throwing dinner
In little baby bits.

What do babies play with?

Pom-poms and bows,   fingers and toes,

Shoes and hats,   sleeping cats,

Frizzy hair,

saggy bear,

Empty box,

Daddy's socks.

What do babies dream of?

Pat-a-cake, pat-a-cake, dickory dock,
Wee Willie Winkie, it's past eight o'clock.

Hey diddle diddle and Little Bo-peep,
Bye Baby Bunting is counting sheep.

What's in a carriage?

diaper bag

favorite rag

food to cook

picture book

floppy bunny

something funny

one shoe

baby too

What are two babies like?

Twins, twins,
Alike as two pins,
Double the trouble . . .

But double the grins!

What is bathtime like?

Babies in a bubble bath,
Building with the bubbles,

Bubbly beards and bubbly hair
And great big bubbly puddles.

What does a baby do?

hug

hold

hide

sleep

smile

slide

jumble juggle jump

bang burp bump

totter tumble throw

gurgle giggle grow

What do lots of babies do?

One baby bouncing on her brother's knee,

Two in a playpen, three by the sea,

Four babies yelling while their
mommies try to talk,

Five babies holding hands,
learning how to walk.

What do *we* do?

Tickle tummies, dry up tears,

Whisper secrets in their ears, then . . .

Bed for baby
And me too,
Bye-bye, baby. I love
You.